# STONE
# COLD

Greg Farshtey – Writer
Jolyon Yates – Artist
Laurie E. Smith  – Colorist

New York

LEGO® NINJAGO Masters of Spinjitzu
#7 "Stone Cold"

GREG FARSHTEY – Writer
JOLYON YATES – Artist
LAURIE E. SMITH – Colorist
BRYAN SENKA – Letterer
NELSON DESIGN GROUP, LLC – Production
BETH SCORZATO – Production Coordinator
MICHAEL PETRANEK – Associate Editor
JIM SALICRUP
Editor-in-Chief

ISBN: 978-1-59707-410-0 paperback edition
ISBN: 978-1-59707-411-7 hardcover edition

Papercutz books may be purchased for business or promotional use. For information on bulk purchases please contact Macmillan
Corporate and Premium Sales Department at (800) 221-7945 x5442.

Printed in the USA
May 2013 by Bang Printing
3323 Oak Street
Brainerd, MN 56401

Distributed by Macmillan

First Printing

# MEET THE MASTERS
## OF SPINJITZU...

JAY

COLE

ZANE

KAI

And the Master of the
Masters of Spinjitzu...

# SENSEI WU

WE DID OUR BEST. WE EACH CHALLENGED A STONE WARRIOR...

AND WE GOT OUR ROBES KICKED!

I USED ALL MY SKILLS AND TRAINING, AND YET I COULD NOT HARM MY OPPONENT.

FOUR TRIES, FOUR FLOPS. LET'S FACE IT, WE'RE JUST *LOSERS!*

NO. YOU ARE MERELY PROUD NINJA WARRIORS, FACING A TRUTH THAT ALL HEROES MUST FACE AT SOME TIME.

WHAT TRUTH IS THAT, SENSEI?

I BELIEVE THERE IS A TALE THAT MUST NOW BE SHARED, BUT FIRST... YOU MUST KNOW THAT I *LIED* TO YOU ALL.

11

"OF COURSE, I KNEW NOTHING OF THIS AS I APPROACHED MY DOJO THAT AUTUMN DAY. THEN I SAW THE NOTE PINNED TO MY DOOR..."

'BEWARE-- ALL YOUR ENEMIES HAVE BEEN UNLEASHED!'

'BUT THESE CLUES CAN HELP YOU TO CATCH THEM AGAIN...'

What is red and blue, covered in feathers, and very, very dangerous?

HMMMMM... THAT'S EASY...

RED AND BLUE WITH FEATHERS AND VERY DANGEROUS...

A PARROT WITH AN AXE!

"THAT TOLD ME WHERE TO GO-- PARROT BAY-- AND WHO I WOULD FIND THERE..."

13

"MY OLD FOE, KIRCHONN THE INVINCIBLE!"

FREE AT LAST!

NOW I CARVE OUT A NEW EMPIRE, BEGINNING RIGHT HERE!

"KIRCHONN ONCE LED A HORDE OF SIX-ARMED WARRIORS, UNTIL I TRAPPED THEM IN THE MOUNT OF SHADOWS."

"BUT EVEN ALONE, HE WAS A DANGER--"

YOU MAY HAVE LOTS OF ARMS, BUT ONLY TWO FEET--

AND THEY ARE NO USE IF NOT ON THE GROUND!

SENSEI WU-- UNNGHH!

I WAS TOLD TO EXPECT YOU.

NOW I HAVE MY REVENGE!

NOT TODAY-- AND NOT UNARMED, AS YOU NOW ARE.

"HE DID NOT DISAPPOINT ME."

YOU WERE A **FOOL**, SENSEI, TO LET ME KNOW WHERE YOU COULD BE FOUND!

YOU HAVE ONLY MADE IT EASIER FOR ME TO DEFEAT YOU.

OR PERHAPS I MADE IT EASIER FOR YOU TO RUSH TO YOUR DESTRUCTION.

I KNEW YOU WOULD SAY THAT. JUST AS I KNOW WHAT YOU WILL SAY NEXT.

THEN I WILL NOT BOTHER SAYING IT. I WILL JUST ACT.

DIDN'T YOU LEARN THE LAST TIME?

YOU CAN'T HIT A MAN WHO CAN SEE YOUR MOVES BEFORE YOU MAKE THEM.

ACTUALLY, I LEARNED MY LESSONS WELL.

YOU MADE ONE MISTAKE, SENSEI-- YOU ARE NOW TRAPPED IN HERE WITH ME.

YOUR POWER LETS YOU DO MANY AMAZING THINGS, TIME NINJA...

UNFORTUNATELY, FLYING IS NOT ONE OF THEM.

YOU SHOULD BE VERY AFRAID, SENSEI. I WOULD BE, IF I WERE YOU... IT WOULD BE THE THING TO DO.

"I WAS SURE THAT WHAT THE TIME NINJA HAD SHOUTED WAS SOME CLUE TO THE IDENTITY OF MY NEXT OPPONENT, BUT I WAS GROWING TIRED AND COULD NOT FIGURE IT OUT."

"I RETURNED TO MY DOJO, FOR I KNEW BOTH MY MIND AND BODY NEEDED REST FOR THE BATTLES TO COME."

"I WASN'T GOING TO GET IT."

HISSSSS

HISSSSS

"SOME DARK FORCE HAD ANIMATED MY STAFF... AND IT WAS STRONGER THAN ME!"

"AND IT WASN'T JUST THE STAFF."

"I HAD TO STOP THE SOURCE OF THIS ATTACK, BUT HOW TO FIND IT?"

BOP

"I DIDN'T HAVE TO WORRY. HE FOUND ME."

BAM

CARDINSTO!

WE MEET AGAIN, OLD FOE.

WITH MY POWER OVER NATURE, I CAN COMMAND THE WOOD OF THE FOREST TO TURN AGAINST YOU. GIVEN TIME, YOU COULD PROBABLY DEFEAT YOUR STAFF, EVEN YOUR FURNITURE...

BUT EVEN IF YOUR POWERS WERE AS NUMEROUS AS THE INSECTS IN THE FIELDS, YOU COULD NOT WIN...

YOU SEE, YOUR DOJO IS MADE OF WOOD, TOO.

CRASH

NO! MY POWER CAN CONTROL THIS... WHATEVER IT IS!

NO EFFECT! HOW CAN THIS BE?

THIS CREATURE EXISTED BEFORE WHAT WE KNOW OF AS THE NATURAL WORLD.

IT IS NOT A PART OF NATURE, SO YOU HAVE NO POWER OVER IT.

SAVE ME! SAVE ME! I DIDN'T MEAN TO KNOCK YOUR HOUSE DOWN, REALLY!

THEN LET'S TALK ABOUT WHO TOLD YOU TO DESTROY MY DOJO.

YOU-- YOU GOT ME!

BUT WHAT ABOUT THAT MONSTER?

OH, I NEGLECTED TO TELL YOU...

THIS PARTICULAR CREATURE CAN ONLY STAY AWAKE FOR 60 SECONDS AT A TIME.

WHOMP

KEEP AWAY FROM ME!

I AM NOT GOING TO HARM YOU... JUST TAKE YOU FOR A *SPIN!*

WHOA! STOP!

I'LL TALK!

I'LL TALK!

THEN ANSWER THIS-- WHO IS BEHIND THESE ATTACKS ON ME?

WHO DESTROYED YOUR PRISON?

I'LL TELL YOU, ONCE THE WORLD STOPS WHIRLING AROUND...

IT'S SOMEONE WHO HATES YOU EVEN MORE THAN I DO.

HE'S NOT GOING TO QUIT UNTIL YOU'RE ANCIENT HISTORY, WU.

WHO IS IT? GIVE ME A NAME!

HIS NAME IS--

"SUDDENLY, THERE WAS A BRIGHT FLASH OF LIGHT, BLINDING ME. I COULD HEAR CARDINSTO'S CRIES, BUT COULD NOT SEE HIM."

NO! HELP!

"WHEN THE LIGHT FADED, MY OLD FOE WAS GONE. ALL THAT WAS LEFT WERE--"

SWORDS... AXES... AND BONES? NONE OF THIS MAKES ANY SENSE!

"NOW I WAS TIRED AND MORE CONFUSED THAN EVER. ALL I WANTED WAS TO GO HOME AND REST."

"I HAD FORGOTTEN THAT MY HOME HAD BEEN WRECKED."

"THAT NIGHT, I LAY UNDER THE STARS, TRYING TO SLEEP AND LOST IN MY OWN THOUGHTS."

"I HAD FOUGHT AND BEATEN ALL OF MY OLD FOES INDIVIDUALLY, BUT NEVER ONE AFTER THE OTHER LIKE THIS."

"SOMEONE WAS TRYING TO WEAR ME DOWN... AND SUCCEEDING."

"MORE, EACH VILLAIN KNEW WHO THE NEXT TO FIGHT ME WOULD BE. KIRCHONN TALKED ABOUT TIME..."

BUZZ

"THE TIME NINJA KEPT USING THE WORD 'WOULD,' TO HINT AT THE 'WOOD' CARDINSTO WOULD USE AGAINST ME..."

"AND THE WIZARD?"

"THEN I REMEMBERED-- 'EVEN IF YOUR POWERS WERE AS NUMEROUS AS THE INSECTS IN THE FIELD.' INSECTS!"

BUZZ    BUZZ

"I TURNED TO SEE A MONSTROUS SWARM OF BEES PURSUING ME. THERE WAS ONLY ONE HOPE OF ESCAPE."

BUZZ

BUZZ

BUZZ

BUZZ

"I RAN AS FAST AS I COULD FOR THE NEARBY RIVER."

"IT NEVER OCCURRED TO ME THAT ONE ENEMY MIGHT BE ALLIED WITH ANOTHER, FOR A JOINT ATTACK."

"I PLUNGED INTO THE WATER, KNOWING THE BEES-- NO DOUBT SERVANTS OF MY OLD FOE, *THE INSECT MASTER*-- COULD NOT FOLLOW ME."

"IF I STAYED UNDERWATER, THE BARRACUDOX WOULD GET ME-- IF I SURFACED, IT WOULD BE THE BEES."

"ONCE AGAIN, I HAD TO CALL ON SPINJITZU TO SAVE ME..."

"WHIRLING FASTER THAN I EVER HAD BEFORE, I CREATED A MASSIVE WATERSPOUT."

"EVEN FOR A SPINJITZU MASTER, TOO MUCH USE OF ITS POWER CAN BE DRAINING."

"AT LAST, I COULD NO LONGER STAY AWAKE AND I FELL ASLEEP BY THE RIVER."

"I SHOULD HAVE EXPECTED A BAD DREAM."

WHERE AM I? WHAT IS THIS PLACE?

YOU'RE WHERE YOU'RE SUPPOSED TO BE, OLD MAN.

IF YOU THOUGHT YOU COULD BEAT ALL YOUR OLD ENEMIES ON YOUR OWN, YOU WERE DREAMING

SO YOU MIGHT AS WELL BE IN THE DREAM WORLD WITH ME.

WHY WOULD YOU BE LIVING HERE, FIRE DRAGON?

HEY, SOMEONE IS ALWAYS DREAMING ABOUT ME.

I'M COOL AND HOT AT THE SAME TIME, RIGHT?

YOU'LL LIKE IT HERE.

THERE ARE SO MANY THINGS YOU CAN DO!

YOU CAN LIE AROUND AND ENJOY THE SUNSHINE, WITH NO WORRIES.

WOULD YOU LIKE SOME ICED TEA?

YOU CAN RIDE ON RAGING RIVERS...

OR RAGE ON RIDING RIVERS...

WHATEVER FLOATS YOUR CANOE.

OR, IF YOU CAN'T BE HAPPY WITHOUT FIGHTING, WE CAN FIND SOMEBODY FOR YOU TO FIGHT...

A LOT OF SOMEBODIES, IN FACT.

AND ALL YOU HAVE TO DO... IS *STAY*.

STAY?

I KNEW YOU WOULD 'WAKE UP' EVENTUALLY... BUT I HOPED IT WOULD BE TOO LATE.

GAHRANN THE DREAMER!

NATURALLY... WHO ELSE COULD ATTACK YOU THROUGH YOUR NIGHTMARES?

OR, FOR THAT MATTER, BE THIS HANDSOME AND CHARMING?

NOW THAT I KNOW IT IS YOU, I CAN ARM MY DREAM SELF. PREPARE FOR BATTLE!

SILLY MORTAL, THAT'S NOT A STICK...

THIS IS A STICK!

NOW, SENSEI, GET READY TO-- HEY! THAT'S NOT FAIR!

GOODBYE, DREAMER.

HOW DID HE KNOW HOW TO DO THAT? I'VE BEEN HERE FOR ETERNITY AND I JUST LEARNED HOW TO DO THAT A MONTH AGO.

YOU WOULD BE SURPRISED WHAT I KNOW.

WHOK

WHAT? NO! NO!

THAT IS NOT A FATE I WOULD WISH ON ANYONE, BUT HE WHO LIVES BY VIOLENCE--

AAAAHHHHHH!

OH, SENSEI...

WHAT--?!

MADE YOU LOOK!

YOU DIDN'T REALLY THINK IT WOULD BE SO EASY TO BEAT ME, DID YOU?

IN THIS REALM, I AM KING, AFTER ALL.

YES, YOU ARE A POWERFUL KING...

SO WHY DO YOU SERVE ANOTHER?

EH? WHAT ARE YOU TALKING ABOUT?

YOU ARE NOT THE MASTERMIND BEHIND THE OTHER ATTACKS ON ME...

THEY WERE TOO SLOPPY FOR A GENIUS SUCH AS YOURSELF.

I CAN'T ARGUE WITH THAT.

BUT YOU ARE WORKING FOR THE SAME BEING MY OTHER FOES WERE...

SOMEONE POWERFUL ENOUGH TO COMMAND A KING?

WHO WOULD THAT BE?

NO ONE GIVES ME ORDERS!

REALLY?

SOMEONE DOES NOW.

GET OFF ME! WITH YOUR WEIGHT ADDED, WE'LL FALL!

SO? THIS REALM IS ENDLESS. WE CAN FALL, BUT NEVER LAND...

AND IT'S NOT THE FALLING THAT IS USUALLY THE PROBLEM, IT'S THE SUDDEN STOP.

YOU FOOL! DON'T YOU REALIZE WHAT LIES AT THE BOTTOM OF THE DREAM WORLD?

THE DREAMS OF... I ALMOST CAN'T BEAR TO SAY IT... HAPPY PEOPLE.

40

44

THAT'S WHAT I SAID.

MAYBE I'M NOT DOING IT FAST ENOUGH.

WHOA! MAKE THE ROOM STOP SPINNING!

WHY DID WE THINK THIS WAS A GOOD IDEA?

"SOMEHOW, I SEEMED TO KNOW MUCH OF WHAT WOULD HAPPEN IN THE FUTURE... OR WAS SUPPOSED TO APPEN. AND, THOUGH I HAD YET TO MEET ANY OF YOU IN PERSON, I ALREADY KNEW OF YOU AND YOUR OTENTIAL. SO YOU CAN IMAGINE MY HOCK AT SEEING THE FOUR OF YOU ASSEMBLED."

WAIT A MINUTE, BUT THEY'RE... AND YOU'RE... YOU'RE--

--GAHRANN!

⟩OOOF!⟨

I HAD YOU GOING THERE FOR A MINUTE, ADMIT IT! BUT IN THE END, YOU JUST AREN'T ANY FUN AT ALL... EVEN IN YOUR DREAMS, THOSE NINJA HAD TO SHOW UP.

SO I AM GOING TO SAY SOMETHING I HAVE NEVER SAID TO ANYONE...

"AND WAKE UP I DID, WITH THE MEMORY OF THAT CRUEL TRICK GAHRANN THE DREAMER HAD PLAYED ON ME."

"I HAD HAD ENOUGH."

"NO LONGER WOULD I WAIT FOR MY ENEMIES TO ATTACK ME. I WOULD TAKE THE BATTLE TO THEM."

"I WOULD STOP THEM BEFORE THEY COULD HOPE TO STOP ME."

"I SAT AND THOUGHT FOR A LONG TIME ABOUT WHAT THE MASK HAD SAID. 'LOOK IN THE MIRROR... IN THE MIRROR...'"

"AND THEN I KNEW."

A MIRROR? OH, NO...

"I RUSHED TO THE NEAREST VILLAGE..."

A MIRROR! MY FRIENDS, PLEASE, SOMEONE GIVE ME A MIRROR.

I FOUND ONE, FINALLY, IN THE WINDOW OF AN ANTIQUE SHOP, AND WHEN I LOOKED INSIDE..."

"I KNEW WHAT I WOULD SEE."

"GARMADON!"

HELLO, BROTHER. HOW NICE TO SEE YOU.

YOU ARE NO BROTHER OF MINE, DARK ONE!

I REALIZED, WHEN THE MASK OF MALICE SPOKE OF A MIRROR, THAT YOU MUST BE THE ONE BEHIND ALL THIS!

OF COURSE YOU DID.

FOR WE BOTH KNOW THAT MIRRORS ARE WINDOWS INTO THE UNDERWORLD, WHERE YOU EXILED ME SO LONG AGO.

BUT LET ME GET A BIT MORE COMFORTABLE...

WHAT ARE YOU DOING? YOU CANNOT EXIST IN THIS WORLD, YOU KNOW THAT.

THIS ISN'T THE REAL ME... JUST A PART OF ME, COME TO GIVE MY BELOVED BROTHER FAIR WARNING.

I HOPE YOU ARE PAYING ATTENTION...

SHOW YOURSELF, BROTHER --YOUR REAL SELF-- AND FIGHT WITH HONOR.

OH, TOO MUCH OF ME IS STILL IN THE UNDERWORLD FOR THAT...

...AND BESIDES, I HAVE NO HONOR.

"GARMADON HAD DISSOLVED INTO THE MIRROR..."

BUT NOW YOU KNOW I AM COMING.

"...AND THE MIRROR BEGAN TO CRACK..."

YOU JUST DON'T KNOW WHEN OR WHERE.

"FINALLY, THE MIRROR **SHATTERED!**"

CRASH

"USING ALL MY SKILLS I WAS ABLE TO DODGE THE SHARDS OF GLASS..."

"GARMADON WAS GONE, LEAVING ONLY THE SHATTERED MIRROR GLASS BEHIND HIM. BUT I WAS DETERMINED NOT TO LET IT END THERE."

"THAT MIRROR HAD BEEN TOUCHED BY HIS POWER. IF I RESTORED IT, PERHAPS I COULD FIND HIM AGAIN."

"WHEN AT LAST I WAS DONE, I DARED TO LOOK INSIDE..."

"AND I SAW... THE FUTURE... A FUTURE FILLED WITH SOME OF THE GREATEST MENACES I COULD IMAGINE."

THAT WAS WHEN I REALIZED... I COULD NO LONGER AFFORD TO FIGHT ALONE.

THE REST YOU KNOW. I RECRUITED AND TRAINED THE FOUR OF YOU FOR THE FIGHT AGAINST GARMADON, AND THE OTHER FOES I SAW IN THAT BROKEN MIRROR.

WELL, WE DON'T KNOW EVERY-THING.

KAI'S RIGHT-- YOU SAW THE FUTURE!

TELL ME, WILL I BE FAMOUS AS THE WORLD'S GREATEST INVENTOR... OR THE WORLD'S GREATEST NINJA?

I THINK THERE ARE MORE IMPORTANT QUESTIONS TO ASK...

LIKE, DID THE SENSEI SEE ANY THREATS BEYOND THE STONE WARRIORS?

IT IS NOT GOOD FOR ANY MAN TO KNOW HIS FUTURE, COLE...

BELIEVE ME, I KNOW. BUT YOU SEEM TO BE MISSING THE POINT OF MY TALE...

EACH OF YOU TRIED TO CHALLENGE THE STONE WARRIORS ALONE, AND LOST.

BUT YOU WERE MEANT TO BE A TEAM. THERE IS NO SHAME IN ADMITTING YOU NEED HELP.

WAS THAT THE POINT? I THOUGHT IT WAS THAT GARMADON IS A REAL--

JAY!

YOU SEEMED TO DO PRETTY WELL ON YOUR OWN, SENSEI.

INDEED. YOU WON ALL THE FIGHTS.

PERHAPS I TOLD IT WRONG...

PERHAPS MY TEAMMATES WOULDN'T GET THE POINT OF A STORY IF THEY SAT ON IT.

AT LEAST IT'S GOOD TO KNOW ALL YOUR OLD ENEMIES ARE WHERE THEY CAN'T HURT ANYONE. RIGHT?

ONE CAN ONLY HOPE.

HEY, IF ANY OF THOSE GUYS SHOW UP, WE'LL POUND THEM... AS A TEAM!

ONE CHALLENGE AT A TIME, JAY, PLEASE? STONE WARRIORS FIRST, EVERYONE ELSE LATER.

COME ON, ZANE, WHERE'S YOUR SENSE OF ADVENTURE?

NEVER THE END.

# WATCH OUT FOR PAPERCUTZ™

Welcome to the Sensei-tional seventh LEGO® NINJAGO graphic novel from Papercutz, the miniature collectible comics company dedicated to publishing great graphic novels for all ages! I'm your humble Editor-in-Chief, Jim Salicrup. Once again I have gathered my special ninja team—consisting of Greg (Red Ninja) Farshtey, Jolyon (Blue Ninja) Yates, Laurie E. (White Ninja) Smith, Bryan (Black Ninja) Senka, and Michael (Green Ninja) Petranek—to tell a tale from the great NINJAGO saga that is unavailable anywhere else.

Y'know, there's a fancy-schmancy term for the type of storytelling that LEGO NINJAGO is involved in— it's called transmedia. That's where an unfolding fictional world is revealed not through just one medium—such as books or TV, but through several all at the same time. The continuing saga of Sensei Wu and his team of Spinjitzu Masters is told not only on TV in the hit Cartoon Network animated series, but in the novels from Scholastic, in the toys (in adventures dreamed up by you, and played out in real 3-D!), and in our graphic novels! In other words, while you can enjoy LEGO NINJAGO in any one medium—TV, prose novels, toys, and comics—you can also more fully experience LEGO NINJAGO by getting it all!

For example, this very graphic novel – LEGO NINJAGO #7 "Stone Cold" by Greg Farshtey and Jolyon Yates—features an exclusive story dealing with Sensei Wu's past that you simply won't find anywhere else! Not on TV or in any prose novel. Obviously this story is set during the time when the Masters of Spinjitzu are battling the seemingly unstoppable Stone Warriors, although Wu's story takes place even before he assembled his ninja team.

Now, if you've already seen all of the animated LEGO NINJAGO animated episodes on Cartoon Network, you may think the saga of Ninjago is done, finished, all over, kaput. Well, let me tell you, that's just not the case! Check out LEGO NINJAGO #8 for an all-new story featuring not only Jay, Cole, Zane, Kai, and Sensei Wu, but Garmadon, and his son Lloyd, as well—that takes place AFTER the animated series! That's right! And the only place you'll find this first post-Stone Warriors tale is right here at Papercutz! Check out the special preview on the very next page!

So, don't despair, LEGO NINJAGO fans—there's still much, much MORE to come!

Thanks,

## STAY IN TOUCH!

EMAIL:      salicrup@papercutz.com
WEB:      www.papercutz.com
TWITTER:      @papercutzgn
FACEBOOK:      PAPERCUTZGRAPHICNOVELS
SNAIL MAIL:      Papercutz, 160 Broadway, Suite 700, East Wing, New York, NY 10038

It has been a month since the defeat of the Stone Warriors. Peace has returned to the world of Ninjago...

But the Ninja know they must keep training, just in case trouble strikes again...

NOW, JAY, I'LL--

HA! KAI, DID YOU EXPECT ME TO WAIT FOR IT?

LET'S SEE HOW YOU LIKE THE PYTHON THROW, AND-- ⇒OOF!⇐... COME ON-- WHY ISN'T THIS WORKING?

MAYBE YOU'RE DOING IT WRONG?

THEY HAVE ACCOMPLISHED MUCH, MY NINJA... BUT THEY STILL HAVE MUCH TO LEARN.

WELL, THEY HAVE AN EXCELLENT TEACHER, MY BROTHER.

PERHAPS I HAVE TAUGHT THEM ALL I KNOW. THEY WOULD BENEFIT FROM A NEW INSTRUCTOR.

ME? WHAT COULD I TEACH THEM, OTHER THAN HOW TO BRING MISERY?

"MY PAST," SAYS GARMADON, "IS NOTHING TO BE PROUD OF IF NOT FOR YOU AND YOUR NINJA, I WOULD HAVE WRECKED THIS WORLD. THE MEMORY OF MY EVIL DEEDS WILL NEVER DIE."

# DESTINY OF DOOM

Greg Farshtey – **Worrisome Writer**

Jolyon Yates – **Anxious Artist**

Laurie E. Smith – **Cautious Colorist**

Bryan Senka – **Leery Letterer**

Michael Petranek – **Apprehensive Associate Editor**

Jim Salicrup – **Expectant Editor-in-Chief**

YES, YOU WERE A DESTROYER, ONCE...

NOW YOU HAVE THE CHANCE TO BE A BUILDER. THE CHOICE IS YOURS.

I TRY AND TRY AND I JUST CAN'T MASTER THAT MOVE!

THERE MUST BE SOME SIMPLE TRICK I AM MISSING.

THERE IS. YOU HAVE TO DROP YOUR RIGHT SHOULDER AS YOU MOVE IN SO YOU CAN GET THE RIGHT LEVERAGE.

WHO ASKED YOU? IN CASE YOU HAVEN'T NOTICED, WE'RE NOT SKELETONS OR STATUES.

WE'RE NINJA!

I KNOW THAT. I WAS SIMPLY TRY-ING TO--

DON'T. JUST DON'T. AFTER ALL YOU'VE DONE, YOU'RE CRAZY IF YOU THINK WE'LL LISTEN TO YOU!

KAI, COME ON, BACK OFF.

I DON'T BLAME YOU FOR HOW YOU FEEL, KAI.

MAYBE MY BEING HERE AT ALL IS A MISTAKE.

Don't Miss LEGO NINJAGO #8 "Destiny of Doom"!